Illustrations by FRANCESCA ROSSI

Classic Fairy Tales by Hans Christian Andersen

WS Kids

WHITE STAR KIDS

Contents

The Little Mermaid

In the ocean, where the water is clear as crystal, where the sea bed lies deepest, stood the castle of the king of the people of the sea. The king was a widower, so it was his aging mother who took care of the princesses, seven lovely mermaids, fascinating creatures whose bodies ended in fish tails. All day, the princesses played in the castle gardens, where each of them had a small flower bed in which she could plant her favorite flowers. One of them planted her flowers in the shape of a whale, another created a floral octopus, but the youngest put in her garden only red flowers and a marble statue of a beautiful young man, which had floated down to them after a shipwreck. The little mermaid was intrigued by the world on land and often asked her grandmother to tell her everything she knew of cities and men! One evening, the grandmother said to her granddaughters, "When you turn fifteen, you will be allowed to go up to the surface." As each of the sisters' fifteenth birthdays came around, they were one by one allowed to surface. On their return, they told the others what they had seen and heard: the beauty of the sunsets, the moon and the stars, cities full of lights and sounds, the changing of the seasons. On many nights, the little mermaid gazed upwards through the water, and if a shadow passed across the light of the moon, she knew that above her was perhaps a passing whale, or a ship with many men, all unaware of her existence. Finally, the long-awaited birthday arrived. The little mermaid took a deep breath and began kicking upward. As she broke the surface, the sun was setting. When it was almost dark, a great ship passed not far from her, and she could hear music and singing coming from it. The little mermaid swam to a porthole and peered inside. She saw that they were having a party for the young prince, who was also celebrating his birthday that day. All at once, the little mermaid heard the roar

of a storm welling up from the depths of the ocean. Within moments, the waves became bigger and a gale blew up. The ship was lifted by the swell, then it crashed back into the sea. The mast broke and the ship crumpled.

The little mermaid saw the prince disappearing into the waves. She swam as fast as she could, she dived and resurfaced many times until she reached the unconscious young man and, holding his head up out of the water, let the currents carry them away. The next morning the storm had passed. There was no trace of the ship, and the prince was still unconscious. The little mermaid kissed his forehead and watched him for a long time, trying to remember where she had seen him before. Then she remembered the marble statue in her garden. The young man looked very much like it! She hoped against hope that he would live. Then she saw the coast before her. On a promontory stood a magnificent building. A grand staircase ran down to the sea, where there was a small creek leading to a white beach. She swam to it and laid the prince on the sand. When she saw some people approaching, she hid and sang a sweet song to attract their attention. That enchanting voice was the first sound that the prince heard when he awoke. The moment the prince and his rescuers moved away, the little mermaid felt a great sadness come over her, so she dived into the water and returned home. Many times after that, she swam back up to the beach where she had left the prince, but she never once saw him, and she returned home each time sadder than the last. Her sisters begged her to tell them the cause of such sadness, so the little mermaid told them every detail of her first trip to the surface. "Maybe I can help you," said her oldest sister, "I know where to find the prince's palace! Come with me." When they arrived at the royal palace, the little mermaid gasped: she had never seen such a marvelous building! It was made of a shiny yellow stone, had large marble staircases, and golden domes rose up from the roof. The little mermaid

returned there many times, edging closer and closer, and she learned not to fear humans any more. In fact, she wished more and more to live among them. There was so much of their world that she would like to learn about, but one thought, more than any other, stayed with her from the moment she saved the prince. So, one day, she asked her grandmother, "If you save a drowning man from death, will he live forever?" "No, my dear, men also die," replied the older mermaid. "But unlike us, who turn into sea foam, humans possess a soul that continues to live and climbs up to the shining stars, to beautiful places that we can never know!" "I'd give a hundred of the years that I have yet to live to be like a human just for one day! Grandmother, is there nothing I can do to have a soul?" she asked.

Her grandmother said, "If a man loved you more than anything in the world and married you. Then, part of his soul would enter your body and you would be able to take part in human happiness. But, little one, you have to stop dreaming about the world of men! Those fools would never welcome you! There is something we consider beautiful that is thought horrible on terra firma: our fish tail. For them, those strange props which they call legs and feet are beautiful. Now, let's see your lovely smile: tonight there is a ball at court. Let's go!" concluded her grandmother, taking her hand.

The throne room was a wonderful sight to behold! Thousands of huge shells, pink and green as grass, were lined up on all sides, and in the middle dolphins danced and mermaids sang sweetly. The little mermaid sang better than anyone, and for a moment she felt happy, but immediately her thoughts turned back to the prince. Quietly, she slipped out of the castle, sure she would never give up the love she felt for him. "This is what I'll do!" she said to herself, herself. "I'll go and visit the sea witch. I have always been so afraid of her, but she's the only one who can help me!" Determined, she went to the cave where the witch lived. She had nev-

er been there before. Nothing grew there: no algae or coral. There was only the gray sandy sea bed, and currents that swallowed up all they took hold of. Beyond these terrible whirlpools was the witch's cave, guarded by hundreds of octopuses, which wrapped themselves around anything that approached. The little mermaid stopped, uncertain. Her heart was pounding with fear, but she thought of the prince and screwed up her courage. She tied back her long hair, so that the octopuses couldn't get hold of her, then passed quickly between the horrible creatures. So she came into the presence of the witch, who told her, "I know what you want: to get rid of your fish tail and have in its place two props so that you can walk like a human, so that the prince will fall in love with you... You must be crazy! Still, I'll make you a potion. You must swim up to the beach and drink it before the sun rises. Then your tail will turn into what humans call 'legs'. But remember," added the witch. "Once you have been transformed into a woman, you can never go back to being a mermaid! If you do not find the prince's love, you will never have an immortal soul, and if he marries another, your heart will break with the pain and you will become foam! Are you sure that this is what you want?"

"I'm sure," replied the little mermaid without any hesitation.

"Very well, but you must pay me, and the cost is not small. You have the most beautiful voice of all the inhabitants of the sea and I want it for myself."

"I accept!" exclaimed the little mermaid. The witch gave her the magic potion, taking her voice as payment. The little mermaid passed through the swarm of octopuses and saw in the distance her father's castle. The grand ballroom was dark now. There's no doubt that if she had known what was going to happen she would have stopped right then! As she swam to the surface, she felt that her heart would break. The sun had not yet risen when she reached the beach. She gazed one last time on her long, shiny tail, then drank the fiery potion. Immediately, she felt an unimaginable heat so intense that she fainted. When the sun rose, she woke up and saw before her none other than the prince, and he was staring at her with a worried frown. The little mermaid looked down and saw that her fish tail was gone. Now she possessed the most beautiful white legs that any girl had ever had! The young man asked her who she was. She looked at him kindly, but could not say a word. He helped her up. For the first time, and not without much pain and difficulty, the little mermaid tried to walk on those strange fins called 'feet'. The girl was very welcome at the palace. She received great care and attention. At the banquet that took place that evening in the throne room, she sat at the royal table. Graceful young women danced and sang before the prince, and the mermaid joined their dance, amazing everyone with her grace.

From that day on, the girl and the prince were inseparable. Together they rode and walked through the woods, sharing long silences filled with emotion.

For the little mermaid, walking was terribly painful, and every step felt like a knife piercing her small feet. So, at night, when no one was looking, she would go to the seashore to seek relief in the cool water. One night, her sisters came to the shore to greet her, singing softly and telling her how much everyone missed her.

The young mermaid was greatly saddened, but this was the life she had decided to live, beside the prince, who loved her more and more every day, and who every day wanted more and more to enjoy her silent company.

Often, he told her that she reminded him of the girl who had saved him the night of the storm, the only one that he would have wanted at his side for life. Imagine the despair of the young woman who could not tell him that it was she had who had saved him from the waves and from certain death! One day the prince said sadly, "I have to leave. I have to meet my future wife," and then, seeing the girl's shocked expression, he added, "I do not want to be separated from you either! Come with me. You are not afraid to go to sea, are you?" That evening the two young people waited on the deck of a ship as the sun went down. "My father has been planning this marriage for months! He agreed to wait until I found the girl whose voice I dream of, but now I understand that I see her only in my dreams. And since I have known you, I cannot help but imagine her with your face. If only we could choose who to marry..." he whispered. He moved closer to the little mermaid and placed a kiss on her lips, then, turning for one last, sad look, he went below decks. As night fell, the little mermaid's sisters came to the surface and swam to the ship, singing.

"Little sister, come home," they begged. But she shook her head, her eyes full of tears. "Do you love him so much?" her eldest sister asked. She nodded in silence.

This was her place, even if she could not prevent the marriage that would end all her hopes and, indeed, her life.

The next morning, the ship sailed into port. There was a triumphant welcome, and a succession of balls and parties followed one another, but the princess only arrived a few days later. She was very beautiful, her skin was delicate and bright, and her beautiful blue eyes were smiling and full of confidence. "It's you!" exclaimed the prince, "You're the one who saved me from the storm." The little mermaid felt her heart breaking. The morning after the wedding she would be dead, turned into sea foam. The following day, the ceremony was celebrated solemnly, then the couple boarded the ship, and were saluted with the roar of cannon. That night, everyone made merry, and the sailors sang and danced for a long time. Even the little mermaid joined the dance, moving with incomparable grace. The pain in her feet cut like sharp knives, but she paid no attention. The pain in her heart was greater. She knew that this was the last time she would see the man for whom she had left her home, for whom she had given up her beautiful voice, for whom she had suffered daily torment without end. This was the last night she would breathe the same air. She stared into the deep sea and up at the starry sky. Eternal night without thoughts or dreams awaited, because she had no soul, nor could she obtain one. Finally, silence fell on the ship. The little mermaid looked eastward, and saw the red glow of dawn. The first ray of sunlight would kill her.

Now she saw her sisters appear among the waves. They were as pale as she was and their beautiful long hair no longer played in the wind. "We've sold our hair to the witch, in return for helping you," they said. "She gave us this dagger. Before the sun rises, you must bury it in the prince's heart. When his warm blood bathes your feet, they will turn back into a fish tail and you will become a mermaid again. Then you can live out your three hundred years of life before you become salty foam. Do it quickly! Soon the sun will rise, and you will die."

The little mermaid went into the tent where the couple were sleeping and saw the beautiful bride lying with her head on the prince's chest. She leaned toward him and kissed his forehead. In the sky, the light of dawn was brightening. She looked at the knife and then once again at her beloved prince. Desperate, she threw the knife far away into the waves, then jumped into the water and felt her body melting into the foam. The sun rose high above the sea but the little mermaid did not feel as though she was dying. The sun was shining wonderfully, and around her flew creatures that were beautiful and ethereal. Their voices sang a melody so sweet and spiritual that no human ear could hear it. In the same way, no human eye could see them. Light and lovely, they were flying in the air without wings. The little mermaid saw that now she had a body just like theirs, and that with the same lightness she was rising ever higher above the foam. "Where am I going?" she asked, and she heard that her own voice sounded sweet and spiritual just like that of the others. "To the daughters of the air!" they answered her. "As you know, mermaids do not have an immortal soul, and cannot obtain one unless they win the love of a human! The daughters of the air don't have an immortal soul either, but they can win one with good works. We are flying to hotter climes to bring relief and refreshment when the torrid air oppresses and kills men. With perseverance, we continue our mission for three hundred years, and we obtain an immortal soul, forever enjoying the eternal happiness of men. You, poor little mermaid, you have wished with all your heart. You, like us, have suffered and endured, and you came to the world of the creatures of the air. Now, if you do good deeds you may win an immortal soul in three hundred years!"

The little mermaid lifted her transparent arms towards the sun and she felt tears in her eyes. Below her, the ship awoke, and came back to life. She saw that the prince and his beautiful bride were searching for her. They looked sadly at the foam, as if they knew she had thrown herself into the waves. Invisible, she kissed the bride on the forehead, smiled at the prince and soared up with the daughters air to where pink clouds floated in the sky. "In three hundred years we will enter the kingdom of God!" whispered one of them. "We may even reach there sooner. Without being seen, we enter the houses of men where there are children. Every time we find a good child who makes his parents happy and deserves their love, the Lord shortens the period of our trial. The child does not know when we come into the house, but when we smile at him for joy one of those years flies away. But if we find a bad and naughty child, then we weep with pain and every tear increases our trials by a day!"

The Princess and the Pea

There was once a prince who wanted to marry a princess, but, under the laws of the kingdom, she had to be without doubt a blue-blooded girl, in short, a real princess. So, the prince decided that he would take a long journey in search of a bride. He traveled his kingdom from north to south, from east to west, but without success. He then ventured into foreign lands and distant countries. He met many young women who claimed to be authentic princesses, but none of them really convinced him. There was always something that left him with doubts. With one, it was the way she behaved, with another it was the way she laughed, and with a third it was her bearing that was not regal enough. So the prince, becoming more and more dejected, continued on his journey around the world. Finally, after months and months of wandering in search of the perfect bride, he decided to return alone to his castle. One evening, the sky began to cloud over and it became increasingly black and threatening. Then the most violent storm for many years burst upon them. The rain fell in cascades, and deafening thunder followed relentlessly on blinding lightning. The roads were deserted, and the people locked themselves up at home, and huddled by their hearths.

Suddenly, and unexpectedly, someone knocked at the door of the castle. When they went to open the door, the king's guards were faced with a trembling girl, her clothes and hair streaming with water. She told them that she was a princess and that she had come from a distant realm. The king and queen looked her over. She certainly didn't look very regal! The queen was suspicious. She thought, "I know a good way to find out if you really are a princess."

Without a word, she went to the room set aside for guests, put a small pea on the bed and covered it with twenty mattresses and twenty thick quilts. Then she went back to the girl, accompanied her to this room, and bade her good night. The princess could not wait to lie down and sleep, but even though she was exhausted from her long and uncomfortable journey, she could not get to sleep. Whichever way she turned, something hard and annoying prevented her from sleeping.

The next morning, she felt even more tired and sore. The king and queen came to her door, asking her if she had slept well. The princess smiled wanly and said, "I'm sorry to say this, but I could not sleep a wink all night. I do not know what it was, but there was something hard in the bed and it gave me painful bruises all over my body! Several times I looked between the sheets to see if there was something, but I found nothing!"

The king and the queen looked satisfied. They had found a true princess for their son. How could they be sure? Simply because only a young woman of royal blood could feel the presence of a pea under twenty mattresses and twenty quilts. Real princesses, you know, have very delicate and sensitive skin.

Now they rushed to the prince and told him what they had discovered: they had finally found the right bride for him!

The young man was very happy because the princess was really beautiful, and her sweet face revealed a kind soul. Without wasting any more time, and this time without any doubt, he asked her to be his wife. The princess happily accepted, and the wedding was celebrated with a lavish ceremony.

And what happened to the pea? It was locked in a case of purest crystal and preserved in the royal museum.

The Tin Soldier

There was once an old man who loved to make toys using anything that came to his hand. One day he found a lead ladle abandoned in a corner, and he decided he would make a tiny toy army. So he made twenty-five toy soldiers. Each one had a rifle on his shoulder, wore a smart red and turquoise uniform, and with a fierce and determined look seemed all ready to march. The old man laid them carefully in a box and put them on sale.

Imagine the surprise and joy of the little boy who received them that Christmas! Right away, he took them out of the box and put them in a row on the table to admire them better. They were all the same, except one, who was standing perfectly erect like others, despite having only one leg. You see, he was the last soldier to be made and there had not been quite enough lead left to finish him off. The child became attached to this one immediately, and the soldier soon became his favorite toy.

On the table with the small army there were many other playthings, but what stood out more than any other toy was a fantastic cardboard castle, complete with a fortified tower. Through its windows you could see the ballroom, richly decorated for the evening. In front of the castle, surrounded by lovely trees, there was a lake, set with a small mirror, on which swam tiny white swans made of wax.

But what attracted your attention was the figure of a little girl with perfect features, standing in front of the main entrance. Like the castle, she was made of cardboard, but she was wearing a beautiful dress and a light veil of blue silk ribbon encircled her shoulders like a scarf. At the center of it shone a silver star, which lit up her beautiful face. She was holding her arms up over her head, and she was balancing on the tip of one foot.

The other leg, stretched upward, was partially hidden by a long skirt. She was a ballerina. As soon as he was taken out of the box, the soldier's attention was attracted by the beautiful maiden and, looking carefully, he thought that, like himself, she had only one leg. Determined to meet her, he hid himself behind a snuff box that lay on the table among the toys, hoping the child would forget him. Indeed, come the evening, the boy hastily put the other soldiers away in the box, without realizing that he had forgotten his favorite one. It was late now, and everyone went to bed. Silence fell over the house, but in this room a great party started, and its guests were all toys. They all laughed and played happily, some played soccer, some played hide and seek, some played blind man's buff; all but the poor soldiers, locked up in their box. In all this confusion, only two figures remained motionless, almost indifferent to fuss: the dancer on her point with her arms raised high and our tin soldier, erect and composed in his uniform. He never looked away from girl, although he could not find the courage to approach her and talk to her.

At midnight, they heard a sharp click, the snuffbox lid opened and out jumped an evil imp. He was also madly in love with the dancer and it took only glance to realize that he had a rival. Mad with jealousy, he arrogantly called out to the soldier, but he did not answer, remaining motionless. This made the imp angry, and he swore that he would get even. He shouted at the soldier, "You'll see: you won't get away with it! I'll find a way to make you pay. No one takes my place near the beautiful girl. Watch your back! My revenge will come when you least expect it and it

will be ter-
rible!"

The following
morning, when the
child awoke, he saw the
soldier out of his box and placed him on the window sill. We will
never know whether the evil imp cast a
spell, or whether it was just a gust of wind, but the fact is that the window suddenly flew open and the soldier fell out. He ended up stuck head first between
the cobblestones, his one leg up and his bayonet down, and the tip of his helmet
driven into the ground.

The boy ran into the street to look for him, but the carriages passing at great speed and the people who thronged the sidewalk hid him from view, and so the poor child was forced to return home, saddened by the loss of his favorite toy. Meanwhile, the first drops of rain started to fall. First, drizzle, and then ever harder, until it turned into a violent downpour, that flooded the streets in a flash.

The storm had just finished when two boys saw the soldier still stuck between the cobblestones. One of the two had an idea: to float him along the rivulets of water that were running into the drains. So, they made a paper boat and put the soldier in it. As soon as they launched their fragile craft on the water it was sucked into the current and ended up in a dark and dangerous sewer. The poor soldier could not see anything and clung to the boat desperately. All at once, a fat sewer rat appeared and threatened him, demanding that he pay a toll. But the soldier did not answer him and, holding his rifle and bayonet firmly in front of him, he passed safely. He was carried onwards for what seemed an eternity, until, at a certain point, he thought he saw a glimmer of light, and began to hope that this perilous journey would soon come to an end. But his misfortunes were not yet over! The stream on which he was sailing was about to plunge into a wide canal, a drop that for our toy soldier was equivalent to Niagara Falls! The crash was terrible: the boat spun around several times, was swamped with water and capsized. The tin soldier fell into the canal, and his only thought was that he would never see his beloved ballerina again. In that exact moment, a huge fish swallowed him in one bite. Inside the fish, it was pitch dark and the space was very small. As luck would have it, soon after, the fish was caught in a fisherman's net, and it was taken to market to be sold.

Fate works in mysterious ways, and, incredibly, the fish was bought by the cook who worked for the little boy's family. Imagine their surprise when the soldier was found in the belly of the fish! Straight away, the child put him back on the table where it had all begun. Everything was in its place, even the sweet ballerina, who was still standing at the entrance of the castle, where nearby the regal swans swam on the mirror lake. The soldier was happy. He looked on the girl with love, and this time she looked back at him with the same tenderness.

In fact, the ballerina had been very worried when she did not see him lined up with his companions and now at last she felt reassured. But, alas, life, as we have said, never ceases to amaze. It is full of surprises.

Shortly afterwards, one of the younger children, to spite his older brother, seized the soldier and threw him into the fireplace, in the midst of the flames. Perhaps the black imp, angry that his rival had returned, had a hand in it.

All hope was lost: the poor thing felt a terrible heat, the color of his uniform was fading and he could not catch his breath. He looked towards the ballerina with sadness and regret, thinking that they might have spent a long life together if only fate had not been so unkind!

The girl returned his look. Her feelings were the same. Once again they were separated!

At that moment, the door burst open and a great gust of wind swept the castle and the ballerina straight into the fire. In a second, the cardboard of which they were made caught fire and a brilliant flame brought an end to their dream. So it was all over?

The following day, as usual, the fireplace was cleaned out, the ashes were collected with a brush and swept into a dustpan.

Thus, unexpectedly, the two were finally together, despite the evil intrigues of the black imp and the twists and turns of capricious fate.

The Emperor's New Clothes

Many years ago, there lived an emperor, who gave so much importance to the beauty and richness of clothes that he spent most of his money on his wardrobe. Nothing mattered more to him than to have the opportunity to show off some new outfit. In the great city in which he lived, it was very busy, and foreigners arrived every day.

One day, a pair of fraudsters arrived. They were posing as skilled weavers who were famous throughout the world, and they boasted that they could weave for the king the most beautiful fabric you could find. Not only would the colors and the design be extraordinarily beautiful, but the clothes made from this fabric would possess unusual properties: they were invisible to the eyes of those who were not capable of the tasks entrusted to them, or who were just very stupid.

"Ah, yes, these would indeed be magnificent clothes," thought the emperor. "With such clothes on, it would be easy to distinguish the clever from the stupid and find out who is not up to the task that I have entrusted to him! I must have these clothes at all costs!"

And so, he gave a fat advance to the two fellows, so that they would lose no time but begin work immediately. They promptly set up two looms and pretended to make a start on the weaving, but in fact the looms were empty. They asked to be supplied with the most precious silk and the finest gold thread, and they popped them into their bags, continuing to work at the empty looms until late into the night.

"I'd like to know where they are with the work," thought the emperor, but it struck him that anyone who was too foolish or who was inadequate to their task would not be able to see the cloth.

He knew that, as far as he was concerned, this was not a problem, but he thought it would be wiser to first send someone else to see how things were going. Now in the city, there was talk of nothing but the wonderful properties of the fabric, and everyone was curious to find out how stupid or incompetent his neighbor was. "I will send my venerable old prime minister to the weavers. His honesty is unquestionable," thought the emperor. "There is no one better to judge the work, because he is intelligent and always tries to live up to his office."

And the good old prime minister went into the room where the two rogues pretended to work at the empty looms. "God help me!" he thought, opening his eyes wide. "I don't see anything!"

However, he was careful not to say it out loud. The two rascals invited him to come closer, and asked him if he appreciated the beauty of the pattern and the range of colors they were using, pointing here and there at the empty loom.

However hard he tried, the poor prime minister could not see anything and, in anguish, he thought, "Poor me! Am I really so stupid? I never thought to be so, but no one really likes to think that of himself. And what if I am not capable of doing my job? No. I cannot report to the emperor that I cannot see the cloth."

Then one of the two fraudsters asked him, "What do you think?"

"Oh, it's really magnificent!" said the prime minister. "What delicate patterns, what refined colors!

I am very impressed by your work and will tell the emperor so!"

"We are so happy!" said the weavers, and began once again to point out the colors and the details of the design. The prime minister listened to them carefully so that he could repeat everything to the emperor, and he did so. The two swindlers asked for more money, more silk, more gold thread to enrich the fabric, and of course it all ended up in their pockets.

Satisfied, they carried on with their deceit, working at the empty loom.

Shortly after the visit of the prime minister, the emperor, impatient, sent one of his highest officials to check the quality of the work and its progress. Everything happened in the same way as had happened to the prime minister: the official looked and looked again, but could not see anything, because the loom was completely empty.

"What do you think? The fabric is magnificent, is it not?" asked the two tricksters, showing him the extraordinary quality of a fabric that was not there.

"But, I'm no fool!" thought the official, "And that means that I must not be fit for office. It seems very odd! In any case, it is better that no one finds out." So, he praised the beauty of the fabric that he really could not see, and declared himself fully satisfied.

"It's really gorgeous work!" he reported to the emperor.

And in the city no one spoke of anything other than this magnificent fabric.

In the end, curiosity got the better of him. The emperor wanted to examine the fabric himself, even though it was still on the loom and not completely finished. Accompanied by a large crowd of courtiers, the prime minister and the high official among them, the emperor went to view the work in progress. The two fake weavers were working now with more vigor than ever, but with neither warp nor weft.

"It's wonderful, isn't it, Majesty?" exclaimed the two officials. "Look at the embroidery and the colors. What refinement! What craftsmanship!" So saying they gestured to the empty loom, thinking that the others were able to see the cloth.

"But what are they talking about?" thought the emperor. "I don't see anything! This is terrible! Am I a fool? Or am I not fit to be emperor? This is the worst thing that could happen to me..."

While he was immersed in these thoughts, aloud he said, "Oh, but it's beautiful! It's just to my liking." He went up to the empty loom, pretending to examine the work, unwilling and unable to confess to not seeing anything.

All those who followed him, looked in the direction of the loom and of course saw nothing. But they all said, "Beautiful! Magnificent!" And they advised him to wear his new clothes for the first time in the gala parade at the next festival. The emperor conferred knighthoods upon the two fraudsters, with the title of Weavers of the Imperial House.

The night before the day of the festival, the two rascals stayed up to work, with

more than sixteen candles lit, so that everyone could see that they were busy finishing the emperor's new clothes. They pretended to take the cloth from the loom. Then they cut the air with tailor's shears, and they sewed with a needle without thread, and finally announced, "There, the clothes are ready!"

The emperor himself appeared, along with his most illustrious knights, and the two scoundrels, raising their hands in the air, as if displaying something, said, "These are the breeches! Here is the jacket! Here is the train!" and so on. "They are light as a spider's web! It seems as if I'm not wearing anything, but this is definitely their greatest virtue."

All the courtiers nodded with conviction, while not one of them saw anything, because there really wasn't anything to see.

"And now, Majesty, if you would deign to undress, we will help you to put on your new clothes before the mirror," said the villains.

The emperor undressed and the two charlatans pretended to hand him the items one by one, helping him to put them on, pretending to pin to his shoulders something that must be the train, and the emperor turned this way and that before the mirror.

"Majesty, they suit you so well!" everyone exclaimed. "What beautiful design! What colors! It is a gorgeous suit of clothes!"

"Your canopy awaits, Majesty, for you to lead the procession!" announced the master of ceremonies.

"I'm ready," said the emperor, "I really look fine, right?" And once again he turned round in front of the mirror, as if to admire his new suit.

The pages in charge of holding the train, bent down, as if to pick up the cloth from the ground. They walked with hands held out in front of them, because they did not want to let it be known that they saw nothing, much less a train to carry. And so the emperor took his place at the head of the solemn procession, under the large canopy, and all the people rushed into the streets and looked out of the windows, exclaiming, "My, but the emperor's new clothes are so extraordinary! What a beautiful train! How wonderful he looks!" In fact, no one wanted to admit that they could see nothing, and so be judged incompetent or unfit for their jobs. The imperial clothes had never before attracted such admiration.

"But he's got nothing on!" a child suddenly called out.

"My goodness! Hear the voice of innocence!" exclaimed the father, and everyone began to whisper to one another, what the child had said.

"He's got nothing on! A child says that the emperor has nothing on!"

"He's got nothing on!" they were finally all shouting.

The emperor shuddered, for he knew that they were right, but in the meantime he thought, "At this point I have to get through this farce and I have to finish the parade." So, he squared his shoulders and stepped out with an even more majestic gait, and the pages kept walking, carrying the train that was not there.

The Snow Queen

One day, the devil made a mirror capable of hiding the good and beautiful things that were reflected, showing instead all that was ugly, and when something ugly was reflected, it became uglier still. If there was a good thought, in the mirror it was transmuted into a bad one. The devil traveled all over the world with the mirror, and in the end there was nothing that had not been reflected and deformed. Still not satisfied, he decided to fly to the gates of heaven. He had almost reached the realm of the angels, when the mirror slipped from his hands and plummeted to Earth, where it broke into millions of tiny pieces. Some took flight and were carried all round the world by the wind, and when they got into the eyes of people, they buried themselves deep, so they could see only the worst side of things. Some shards worked their way into people's hearts, turning them to ice.

The two young people at the center of our story lived in a very poor neighborhood and their houses were so close that, where the two roofs met, the gutters joined. It was enough to hop over them to pass from one attic to another. Their parents had hung wooden boxes from the windows and in them they had planted herbs and fragrant roses, and the two friends would sit near them to play. They loved each other very much, and they were inseparable! He was called Kay and she was Gerda. One cold winter's day, Kay's grandmother, to distract them said, "Look! You think these are snowflakes, but to me they seem to be large white bees!"

"Do they, too, have their own queen bee?" asked Kay.

"Certainly!" his grandmother said. "Sometimes she flies over the city and looks in through the windows, which then freeze in the strangest way, as if they were covered with flowers."

One evening, Kay pulled up a chair to the window to watch the snow, and suddenly

he saw two big flakes slide toward him. The largest of these fell into one of the boxes of flowers and began to grow until it turned into a beautiful woman, wrapped in white veils that seemed to consist of a snowstorm. Kay was frightened and jumped down from the chair, while a whirlwind transformed the woman into a huge white bird, which took flight. By the next morning, though, Kay had convinced himself that he had dreamed it. When spring finally returned, the children made a habit of meeting in their own little garden between the roofs. One day, while reading a book, Kay said, "Ouch! I've got something in my eye!" Gerda tried to help him, but she could see nothing. In fact, one of the shards from the magic mirror had got into the child's eye and another had worked its way down to his heart. Soon it would become ice! "Why are you making that face?" Kay rudely asked Gerda, "And now why are you crying?" The girl ran home in tears, while Kay, left

alone, realized that he could suddenly see details that he had never noticed before! "That rose has been ruined by worms! The other one's crooked! In fact, those roses are just horrible!" When winter came round again, Kay seemed very happy. One day he stole his grandmother's glasses and, hanging them out of the window he waited for the snowflakes to settle on them. "Look how beautiful, Gerda!" he exclaimed, showing her how, thanks to the lenses, each flake looked larger and just like a flower. Then he ran out of the house with his sled on his back. In the square, the boys were having fun, secretly hitching their sleds to the wagons of the farmers and letting themselves be dragged along. He was playing at this when he came upon a large white sleigh, on which sat a person wrapped in a white fur coat and with her face covered by a hood. The sleigh stopped and Kay took the opportunity to tie his little sled to it. As soon as he had tied the last knot, the sleigh sped off. The driver nodded affectionately to Kay, as if they already knew each other. Unable to untie his sled, the child clung with all his strength and soon they left the city behind. He tried again to untie the rope, but to no avail. Kay was terrified! The snowflakes that were falling grew larger and larger, until it seemed to Kay that he was surrounded by large white birds. Suddenly the sleigh came to a halt. The driver stood up and pushed back her hood, and Kay recognized the woman he had seen out of the window of his room! It was the Snow Queen. She took the child by the hand, made him sit beside her on the sleigh and wrapped him in the hem of her white bear fur. "Are you still cold?" she asked, kissing him on the forehead. Kay shuddered; that kiss was colder than ice! For a moment he seemed almost to die, but then he felt better. When the Snow Queen gave him a second kiss, something terrible happened. Kay forgot little Gerda, and everyone he had left back home. The Queen urged the sleigh into the air and it flew unerringly through the snowstorm that was now raging. As dawn broke, Kay was asleep at the feet of the Snow Queen.

You can imagine how Gerda felt when Kay did not return! She asked everyone in the town if they had seen him, but no one could give her an answer. Some boys remembered seeing him tie his sled to a magnificent sleigh, but their memories were inexplicably confused. In short, no one knew where the boy had gone or who he had gone with. In the end, they said that Kay must have fallen into the frozen river and that she had to resign herself to it. So she stopped looking for him. Gerda wept for a long time over the disappearance of her friend. Then, the cold passed again and spring arrived, bringing with it beautiful warm sunshine. It was to the sun that Gerda turned one morning, as she sat alone, among the roses. "Kay has drowned."

"No, I do not believe it!" answered the sun.

"I tell you he is dead! Gone!" replied Gerda.

"No, we don't believe it!" said the swallows and so, eventually, Gerda too stopped believing it, and she decided to go in search of her friend. She traveled for a long time, questioning the flowers and the stars, but they all answered that they knew nothing.

Months passed, and Gerda found herself alone, far from home amid the cold of winter, but she kept on, trying to stop shivering and shake off her sadness. One day she had stopped to rest by the side of a road when a crow hopped across the snow in front of her. "Caw, caw! Good morning!" he said, and he asked how she came to be all alone in the world. Gerda told the crow what had happened and asked if he had seen Kay.

The bird said, "Could be. I think that a child I met could be little Kay, but certainly he has now forgotten you for the princess."

"He lives with a princess?" asked Gerda.

"Yes. Let me explain! In this kingdom, there is a very clever princess who is terribly bored. One day she thought to herself that if she were not always alone, maybe she would not be so bored. So she decided to find a husband. But she desired a person who could join her in conversation and who would not bore her.

The following day she announced that every handsome young man was invited to the palace and that the one who showed himself the most intelligent would be her husband! A large crowd descended upon the palace, but finding a husband for the princess was not so easy, because everyone became tongue-tied in her presence and not a single one could get a word out!"

"But, Kay?" Gerda asked. "When does he come into it?"

"All in good time!" cried the crow. "It was on the third day that the princess received suitors, when a young boy appeared. His eyes sparkled and he had beautiful long hair, but he was dressed like a peasant."

"It was Kay!" cried Gerda, happily.

"He had a bundle on his back," said the bird.

"That would have been his sled!" said Gerda.

"When he arrived at

the palace, he was not at all intimidated and walked quietly into the presence of the princess, who sat on the throne, bored. He had not come to ask for her hand, he said, but only to find out how intelligent she was. He soon learned that she was extraordinary, and she found him extraordinary too."

"I'm certain it was Kay!" exclaimed Gerda. "Can you get me into the palace?"

"It's not possible. The guards would not allow it," said the crow. "But my sister, who works at the palace, knows a little back door which leads to the princess's bedroom." When the palace lay in darkness, the bird led the girl to a back door, which was ajar. They went in and climbed an imposing staircase, at the top of which they found the tame crow, and she led them to the royal chamber. Gerda went to the bed, lifted a corner of the sheet and saw dark hair. Excited, she called out Kay's name and woke up the prince.

What a disappointment it was to discover that the young man was not Kay! The princess also woke up and demanded to know what was going on. Then the little girl began to cry and told her whole story. Moved, the princess gave Gerda clothes that were both warm and elegant, and placed a golden carriage with the royal crest at her disposal. So the child resumed her journey, but after a while the carriage was attacked by vicious bandits who mistook Gerda for a rich noblewoman and took her prisoner. The child was taken to the bandits' lair where she met their leader's daughter. She was ugly and clumsy, and her ways intimidated Gerda. She showed her the doves that she was holding captive in small cages and her reindeer, tied to the wall with a golden ring through its the nose. Gerda told her story, while the robbers sang and drank around the fire. When everyone was asleep, the doves said, "We have seen little Kay. He was sitting in the carriage of the Snow Queen, heading for Lapland, where she has her palace, perpetually covered with ice. Ask the reindeer who once lived there."

The reindeer answered, "I remember my home, yes, but the Snow Queen's palace is on an island near the North Pole. If she has taken your friend, for sure she will have taken him there."

In the morning, Gerda told the bandit leader's daughter what the doves and the reindeer had said. The young woman ordered the reindeer to conduct Gerda to the Snow Queen's palace. The animal carried Gerda for hours without stopping, through the woods, past the steppes and marshes, going as fast as he could, until they arrived in Lapland. Here they found hospitality with a powerful sorceress, who, after hearing Gerda's story, said, "Little Kay is indeed at the Snow Queen's palace, but he is not a prisoner, at least not in the way you think. He is happy to stay there because there are shards from the devil's mirror in his heart and in one eye," and she explained the story of the mirror.

"The fragments must be re-moved, otherwise the Snow Queen will retain her power over him for-ever."

"But can you help Gerda with a potion or an amulet, perhaps?" the reindeer asked. "I cannot give her a force greater than she already has! She is the only one who can hope to be able to remove the glass from Kay's heart. Two miles from here begins the Snow Queen's garden. Accompany Gerda there and leave her next to a big red berry bush, but hurry back!"

The reindeer galloped off and did not stop until he came to the great bush. There he paused to let the girl dismount, and then he ran away as fast as he could. Alone, Gerda walked through the garden, until suddenly she saw approaching a whole regiment of snowflakes. At least that's how they seemed, for they were not falling from the sky, which was clear and serene. The flakes ran straight into the middle of the garden, getting bigger and bigger, alive and terrifying. They were the soldiers of the Snow Queen and they had the strangest forms. Some looked like horrible hedgehogs, others resembled coiled snakes with their heads poised to strike, still others looked like bears with bristling hair, and all seemed very threatening! Gerda, frightened, began to recite a prayer out loud. The cold was so intense that she could see her breath in front of her. At first, it seemed like smoke, but then it became more dense and turned into small transparent angels which grew larger and larger until they touched the ground. Each one wore a helmet on his head and carried a sword and a shield. In a few instants they had multiplied until they became a whole legion encircling her and protecting her. With their swords, the angels struck out at the snowflakes and sliced them to pieces and so Gerda was able to go on, protected and full of courage, until she reached the Snow Queen's palace. The child entered the palace through a great gate. In front of her there was a grand staircase, its steps cut out of a frozen waterfall. This ascended to the floor above, where there were more than one hundred rooms illuminated by the aurora borealis, all vast, empty, frozen. Right in the middle of the last room there was a

frozen lake fragmented into a thousand pieces, and in the center of this was the Snow Queen's throne and here every day sat little Kay.

The boy's face and hands were purple with cold, but he did not notice. With a kiss, the Snow Queen had seen to it that he did not suffer from the cold. She had made his heart hard as ice and had made him forget everything about his previous life, including his little friend. When Gerda saw him, Kay was sitting at the foot of the throne. He was trying in vain to make the word "eternity" from the fragments around him. The Snow Queen had told him that if he managed to do it he would have become master of himself and she would give him the whole world.

"I have to leave," said the Queen. "I have to go to the warm countries to bring them snow and ice." With that she flew away leaving Kay alone. Now Gerda ran to him and embraced him, but he was immobile, rigid. Little Gerda cried hot tears and these fell on his chest and entered his heart. They melted the block of ice within and corroded away the sliver of mirror that was lodged within. Kay looked at her and then he too burst out crying. He wept so much that the tiny grain of mirror came out of his eye, and now he shouted for joy. "Gerda, where have you been all this time? And where have I been?" he asked, looking around in fright. The scene was so touching that even the fragments of ice began to dance around the pair, forming the letters that the Snow Queen had told Kay to complete, so becoming master of himself and obtaining from her the whole world. The Snow Queen could come back whenever she pleased. The goodbye letter was written there at the foot of the throne in pieces of shimmering ice. The two children joined hands and left the palace, talking without stopping of Kay's grandmother and of the roses on the roof, and where they walked the wind dropped and the sun shone. When they reached the big red berry bush, they found the reindeer waiting together with another reindeer, his companion.

The two animals carried Kay and Gerda to the borders of their country and here bade them farewell, and soon the children were walking on the path through the woods.

From behind a great oak tree one of the horses that had drawn the golden carriage appeared, ridden by a girl with a red cap on her head and a pair of pistols in her hands. It was the bandit leader's daughter. "Ah, so it was for you that this girl traveled half a world!" she said to Kay. "I hope you're worth the trouble she took!" The two recounted what had happened, and when they had finished, the bandit leader's daughter hugged them tightly and then set off to explore the big wide world.

Little by little as the children got closer to home they saw that spring was bursting forth all around them and they greeted it laughing.

When they arrived in their hometown they went to Kay's grandmother's house, ran up the steps and, all smiles, entered the room where nothing had changed. But they had changed. As they crossed the threshold, in fact, they realized that they had grown up! The roses that climbed across the eaves were in flower. Kay and Gerda had already forgotten, as if it were just a bad dream the cold and empty palace of the Snow Queen. They went up to the roses and smiled, and at last the warm summer arrived.

The Tinderbox

A soldier was once marching along the road with a backpack on his back and his sword at his side, on his way home from the war. As he passed through the forest, he came upon an old woman, who said to him, "Would you like a heap of money?"

"Certainly," replied the soldier.

"Do you see that tree?" the woman continued. "It is completely hollow. Climb to the top and then slip down inside. First, I'll tie a rope around your waist, so that I can pull you up again."

"Why do I have to go down into the tree trunk? What will I find there?" asked the soldier.

"A lot of money!" replied the witch. "When you get to the bottom, you will find yourself in a large room illuminated by hundreds of lamps. In front of you, you will see three doors, each with a key in the lock. If you open the first, you come into a room, and in the center you will see a large trunk, on which sits a big dog with eyes as big as saucers. Do not be afraid: spread my apron out on the floor and put the dog on it, then open the chest and take all the coins you want. But, as you will see, they are only copper coins. If you prefer silver, you must go into the second room. There, too, you will find a chest. On this chest sits a dog with eyes as big as millstones. Put him on my apron, and take all the money you want! But if you want gold coins, enter the third room, where you will find a dog with eyes as big as the Round Tower of Copenhagen! Spread my apron on the floor and put him on it. He will give you no trouble and you will be able to take all the gold coins you want!"

"And what do you want in return?" asked the soldier.

"I do not want money. But you must bring me an old tinderbox which my grandmother left there the last time she fell into the tree."

"I promise. Tie the rope around my waist and give me your apron," replied the soldier. He climbed up the tree, then he let himself slide into the trunk, until his feet touched the ground. As the witch had told him, he found himself in a large room. He opened the first door, put the dog on the apron and filled his pockets with copper coins. Then he went into the second room, where he found the second dog, laid him on the apron, got rid of the copper coins and filled his pockets and backpack with silver coins. Then came the third room. The dog that he found there was terrifying, but the soldier laid him on the apron and opened the trunk full of gold coins. He hastily threw away the silver, and filled his pockets, backpack, cap and boots with gold coins. Happy, he closed the trunk, put the dog in his place and called to the witch.

"Have you found the tinderbox?" she asked.

"I forgot, but I'll look for it now!" and he ran to find it.

When the witch pulled him up, the soldier asked her why she wanted the tinderbox, but the old woman told him not to be curious. The soldier threatened her, but the witch would not tell him anything. Then he cut off her head, took the tinderbox back, put the gold in her apron and went to the nearest town. The next day he went to the tailor and bought the most elegant clothes available. The nobility of the region vied to know him, to show him around the city and they told him about the king and his beautiful daughter.

"Where can I go to meet her?" asked the soldier.

"No one can! She lives in a castle surrounded by high walls and towers. The king guards her jealously because according to a prophecy the princess is destined to marry a common soldier, which is for him unthinkable!" they answered.

In the next few days, the soldier continued to enjoy his new life, but money doesn't last forever and he soon found himself with only a few coins in his pocket. So he was forced to move to a miserable attic. One evening, wanting to light a candle, he remembered the tinderbox. He made a spark by striking the flint, and the moment he did so the door flew open and in came the big dog with eyes like saucers. "What are your orders, master?" he asked.

The soldier ordered the dog to bring him some money. The dog disappeared, to return soon after with a bag full of copper coins. It did not take long before the young man found out how the tinder box worked. If he struck once, the dog who guarded the copper coins appeared. If he struck twice, the dog who had been sitting on the trunk full of silver arrived, and three strikes brought the dog who guarded the trunk full of gold coins. The soldier was thus able to resume his life of luxury. However, there was a thought that he could not get out of his head. He wanted to see the princess at all costs. So, one day he struck the tinderbox and made the dog with eyes as big as saucers appear. He ordered him to fulfill his wish. The dog went off and soon returned with the sleeping princess. She was so beautiful that the young man could not help but kiss her. Then he commanded the dog to take her back to the castle. The following morning the princess told her parents a strange dream she had had, about a dog who had carried her on his back, and a soldier who had kissed her. Suspicious, the king and queen ordered the ladies of the court to keep watch at the princess's bedside. As the previous night, the soldier called the dog and ordered him to bring the princess, but one of the ladies managed to follow him. With a piece of chalk, she drew a cross on the door of the house and returned to the castle. Later, when he was taking the princess back to her bedchamber, the dog saw the cross and he drew the same thing on all the doors of the city, so the next day it was not possible to identify the right one. So, the queen took a bag, filled it with flour, and sewed it to the princess's back. She made a small hole so that the flour would run out along the way. After nightfall, the dog came back to pick up the princess, but this time he did not notice the flour, so the next day it was easy to find the house of the soldier, who was arrested and sentenced to be hanged. The following morning, through the bars of the cell, the poor man saw a large crowd gathering to watch the execution. He was in luck and was able to get the attention of a boy and he asked him to go get the tinderbox from his room in exchange for four coins. Enticed by the reward, the boy obeyed. Meanwhile, the gallows was already erected: the king and queen, counselors and judges came to witness the execution. Once on the scaffold, the soldier addressed the king and queen. "If I am allowed one last wish, I would like to smoke one last pipe".

The king agreed, and the soldier took the tinderbox and struck three times. Suddenly, the three dogs appeared! "Save me!" cried the soldier, and the dogs threw themselves on the judges and the counselors, hurling them so high that there was no escape. The same fate befell the sovereigns. Now everyone present was terrified, and they cried out, "We want you as our king." They hauled him into the king's coach, and, preceded by the three dogs, they went to the royal palace. The princess was very happy to be set free from the castle where her father had imprisoned her and the soldier did not mind either. The wedding was celebrated with great pomp and the two young people lived a long life, happy and content, protected and defended by the three dogs with large eyes.

The Wild Swans

In a distant land, there lived a king with eleven sons and one daughter, Elisa. Their days were serene but their happiness was not to last forever. The father, a widower for many years, in fact, decided to remarry. He chose a very wicked woman, who could not abide the presence of her stepchildren. So, she farmed Elisa out to a family of farmers in the country, and talked so badly about the princes that their father no longer wanted to know them. The queen turned the eleven boys into eleven magnificent wild swans and ordered them to fly away forever. Many years passed, each one sadder than the next. Finally, the princess's fifteenth birthday arrived, and she was brought back to the castle, but as soon as the stepmother saw how beautiful she had become, she began to hate her. At dawn one day she went to the big pool that was the girl's favorite place. She took three toads and ordered the first, "Jump on Elisa's head and make her as stupid as you!" To the second she said, "Jump on her face and make it as ugly and unpleasant as you." Finally, she gave this order to the third toad: "Climb onto her heart and make it so bad that her life is nothing but suffering." Satisfied, she put the three toads in the water. However, things did not go as she had planned. As soon as the three toads came into contact with the girl who was so pure and good, they were transformed into beautiful roses. At the height of her anger, the queen threw herself on Elisa. She smeared her with soot, anointed her with a smelly ointment and matted her hair, until she was unrecognizable, even to her father. Desperate, the princess ran away. She ran without stopping, arriving at last in the woods. She was so tired that she leaned her back against a tree and fell asleep. When she awoke, she bathed in the clear waters of a lake, combed her hair and went on her way. She had not gone far when she met an old woman. Elisa asked her if she had seen eleven princes, and

the old woman replied, "I have not seen eleven princes riding in the woods, but I remember seeing eleven swans with crowns on their heads swimming in the river. If you want, I can take you there." When they came to the river, the girl thanked the old woman and walked along it, until it ended in a beach. As the sun set, she saw eleven white swans with golden crowns on their heads gliding toward the shore. Elisa, hidden, began to observe them and, when the sun disappeared into the sea, she saw their coats of feathers drop away and they became her brothers. Joyfully, she rushed into their arms, and together they began to laugh and cry. The oldest brother explained that during the day they were swans, but as the sun went down they turned into men. Then he added, "For this reason we always have to take care to be somewhere we can set foot on terra firma at sunset. In fact, if at that time we were still flying in the sky, becoming men, we would fall to our deaths. Now we live in a far country, and only once a year are we allowed to return home. The journey is long. We have to cross the sea and there is only a rock on whi- ch we can rest for the night, but it is so small that we barely fit in our human form."
When morning came the

princes turned into swans and flew away, to return after dark and take on human form once more. "Tomorrow we must leave and we cannot return for a year, but we do not want to leave you here! Do you want to come with us?" they asked.

"Yes, indeed, I beg you, take me with you!" exclaimed Elisa.

All night they worked, weaving a net out of willow bark and reeds. When it was ready, Elisa lay on it and her brothers, turning into swans at sunrise, took hold of the net with their beaks, and rose up into the clouds. They flew all day, somewhat slowed by the weight they had to carry. Meanwhile, time was passing fast, and evening was approaching. Anxiously, Elisa watched the sun setting, and the rock was nowhere in sight. Once the sun set, her brothers would become men and fall into the ocean. The sun was on the horizon. Elisa's heart trembled, then, finally, she saw the tiny rock. Her foot touched the it just as the sun disappeared into the sea. Elisa looked around and saw that her brothers were holding her in their hands. The following day, at dawn, the swans continued their flight. As the sun rose higher, Elisa saw before her a mountain hanging in the air. Glaciers glittered among the rocks and in the center stood a magnificent castle, surrounded by imposing colonnades, and by forests of palm trees and beautiful flowers. Elisa asked if this was their new home, but the swans shook their heads. What she was seeing was Morgan le Fay's ever-changing castle of clouds. The journey continued for an age, but just before sunset, Elisa found herself on a rock hidden behind creepers.

"I wonder what we will dream tonight!" said the youngest of the brothers.

"I wish I could dream how to save you!" said the girl, then, exhausted, she fell asleep. She seemed to fly up to Morgan le Fay's castle of clouds.

She saw the enchantress come to meet her, beautiful and sparkling, and yet so much like the old woman she met in the forest. "You can save your brothers, but you must be very strong and tenacious, because you will have to endure much

pain and face many fears," said the fairy. "See these nettles? They grow near the cave where you are sleeping or among the graves of the cemetery. You will need to pick them and even if they burn your skin horribly, make them into yarn, and from the yarn weave eleven tunics. Throw the tunics over the eleven swans. This is the only way to break the spell. But remember, from the moment you start work, even though it may take years, you must no longer speak. A single word will bring about your brothers' death!"

When she awoke, Elisa found nettles next to her bed. She left the cave and began her work. The nettles stung the skin of her hands and arms, but she did not stop. She trod each nettle plant with her bare feet, so producing the yarn she needed for her weaving. When her brothers saw what she was doing, they were frightened for her, but then they realized that she was paying the price for their salvation. Elisa worked all night and managed to finish one tunic. Suddenly, she heard the blast of hunting horns and the barking of dogs. Terrified, she took refuge in the cave, taking with her the nettles she had collected. A short time later, the hunters appeared. Among them was the king of that distant country. The young man entered the cave and was stopped short by the sight of Elisa. He had never seen such a beautiful girl!

"Where are you from?" he asked. Elisa shook her head without saying a word. "Come with me!" the king told her, "You will be my queen." And so saying, he made her get on his horse and they rode off toward the royal palace. Disconsolate, Elisa wept throughout the ride, without being able to say anything. At the castle, the ladies dressed her in royal clothes, adorned her with beautiful jewels and covered the wounds on her hands with soft gloves. Elisa looked gorgeous! The king introduced her to everyone as his future bride, but she did not smile and she never spoke a word. Then the king opened the door of a room near Elisa's bedroom. On the floor she saw the threads she had extracted from the nettles and the

one tunic she had finished. As soon as she saw them, Elisa smiled and kissed the
king's hand. Despite the opposition of the archbishop, who suspected the future
queen of witchcraft, the marriage was celebrated with great solemnity. The king
loved his wife, but could not understand her behavior. Every night, the
young woman left him and went into her private room, where
she wove one tunic after another. She had already completed six, when she ran out of material. The enchantress
had told her that the nettles she must use grew in the
cemetery, so she decided to go there as soon as night
fell. Unfortunately, the archbishop saw her and tried to convince the king that his suspicions were well
founded. Many more days and nights passed, and the
young woman had almost finished her work, but she
once again found she had run out of nettles. Reluctant-
ly, she decided to return to the cemetery. This time, however, the king and the archbishop followed her. Faced with the
evidence, the king could not do anything and Elisa was brought
before the court, tried for witchcraft and condemned to die at the stake.
She was taken to prison and as bedding they gave her the rough nettle tunics. She
began working immediately, still in silence, and without any way of explaining
or defending himself. Towards evening, her brothers arrived. This was perhaps
the last time she would see them, but the work was almost finished and they were
close to her. She had just one more night to finish the last shirt. Desperate, the
eleven brothers asked to be received by the king. They threatened and begged,
but there was nothing to be done, and as the sun rose again they became swans.
All the people flocked to the city to see the burning of the witch. Elisa arrived on

a cart, dressed in a shabby cloth tunic: not even then did the girl stop sewing. The people insulted her and some rushed at her to take away the work that seemed to be so important to her, thinking it must be part of an evil spell. Then, from above, came eleven swans, and they surrounded the cart, beating the crowd away with their wings. The people fled in terror. The executioner managed to grab Elisa's hand, but now she was hurriedly throwing eleven tunics over the swans. The creatures immediately changed into their human form. The youngest, however, bore a wing instead of an arm. His sister had not had time to finish his tunic.

"Elisa is innocent!" cried the eldest brother and told the whole story. Moved, the people bowed down in front of her as if she were a saint. Freed from her oath, the girl was able to explain everything to her husband and to tell him she loved him and forgave him for having suspected her. From that day on they all lived happily together at the castle, far away from their sad memories.

The Nightingale

The emperor of China's palace was the most beautiful in the world, entirely built from the finest porcelain. The garden was wonderful as well. Silver bells had been attached to each flower and they tinkled gently in the wind and the garden was so vast that it was impossible to come to the end of it. If you continued to walk for a long time, you would come to a beautiful forest with tall trees and crystal-clear pools. The forest ran down to the sea, so travelers, sailors and fishermen could sail in the shade of the trees, listening, enraptured, to the melodious song of a nightingale who lived among the leafy branches. Though enchanted by the splendor and wealth of the royal palace, everyone who visited talked about nothing but the nightingale when they returned home. The talk reached the ears of the emperor who called his lieutenant and his counselors and asked about this wonder, but none of them knew anything. Annoyed, the emperor ordered the nightingale to be brought to court immediately. The lieutenant asked everywhere for news of the melodious bird and finally, just as he had begun to despair and fear imperial punishment, he found a young girl in the kitchen who said, "I know the nightingale. She lives near the beach and sings divinely."

So everyone made their way into the woods, and when the girl finally pointed to a bird perched on a branch, the lieutenant, a little disappointed by her dull appearance, addressed her solemnly, "Little nightingale, our great emperor wishes you to sing for him!"

"Gladly," said the nightingale, and filled the air with her wonderful melodies.

The lieutenant, shaking off the music's enchantment, announced, "I have the pleasure of inviting you to a celebration this evening at court, where you will delight our beloved sovereign with your singing!"

At the palace, great preparations for the evening were under way. All the courtiers in their sumptuous clothes were present, and in the middle of the great hall, next to the emperor's throne, a golden perch was placed for the nightingale. She sang so well that night that the even the emperor was moved to tears, and he decided that from that day the bird would remain at court, in a golden cage. She would be permitted to fly twice a day and once at night, but tied to twelve silk ribbons held by twelve servants. One day, a large parcel was brought to the emperor, on which was written: "NIGHTINGALE". Inside was a small nightingale, but it was mechanical and was covered with diamonds, rubies and sapphires. As soon as it was wound up, it began to sing, moving its golden tail. Around its neck was a ribbon, on which was written: "The emperor of China's nightingale is a poor thing compared to that of the emperor of Japan." Everyone was enchanted, and the emperor desired that the two birds, the real one and the one mechanical one, would sing together in a beautiful duet. Actually, things did not go very well, so they had them sing separately. Both were very good, but the mechanical nightingale received greater acclaim since it was also so beautiful to look at, as it sparkled with gold and precious stones.

It sang thirty-three times, and always the same melody, always perfectly, and people would gladly have heard it again, but the emperor declared his desire to hear the real nightingale... but where was she? Seduced as they were by the song of the mechanical nightingale, they had not realized that the bird had flown out the window, toward the woods.

After a moment of surprise and dismay, they all agreed that, after all, the mechanical nightingale was far better than the real thing, and they proceeded to listen to the same melody for the thirty-fourth time.

The master of the emperor's music got permission to show the bird to the people. Thus, the following Sunday, everyone listened and praised the song of the mechanical nightingale. Everyone, that is, except the fishermen who had been lucky enough to enjoy the melodies of the real bird, and they did not find the mechanical bird's performance so very impressive. The real nightingale was banished from the empire, and the artificial bird was placed on a silk cushion close to the emperor's bed, and was awarded the title of 'Imperial Singer'. So, a year passed, and the emperor, his courtiers and all the Chinese learned by heart every note of the artificial bird's song and sang it all the time.

One evening, while the artificial bird was singing for the emperor as he lay in his beautiful royal bed, it produced a strange metallic sound, and then the music stopped altogether. The emperor sprang out of bed, and called his doctor, who could do nothing. Then he called the watchmaker, who with great difficulty somehow repaired the bird, but said that the emperor must use it as little as possible because its parts were now worn out and he could not replace them. With great regret, the emperor decreed that he would listen to the mechanical bird only once a year, in order to preserve its song.

Five years passed, and the whole country was deeply saddened by the state of health of their beloved emperor, who was seriously ill. He would not live much longer, and a new ruler had already been chosen. One terrible night, the valets found the emperor pale and cold in his big bed. Believing him dead, they ran to hail the new emperor. In the sumptuous halls and corridors of the royal palace, the floors were covered with heavy carpets, so that every noise was muffled and silence reigned everywhere.

The emperor, however, was not dead yet. The window of his room was open, allowing the silvery light of the moon to fall on him and on the precious mechanical nightingale.

The emperor was breathing with difficulty and now saw death, who, sitting on his chest, wore a gold crown on his head, resplendent with precious stones. In one hand he held a golden sword and in the other a beautiful banner. Around them, among the folds of the heavy velvet curtains, strange figures appeared, some frightening, some sweet and tender; they were the emperor's actions, both good and bad, and they were watching him now that death was imminent. "Do you remember?" they whispered one after the other.

"Do you remember?" And they told him so many things, so many evil deeds and so many injustices that the emperor had committed but which he did not even recall. He was so frightened that sweat ran from his frozen forehead and he asked with the little voice he had left, "Music! I want the music of the great Chinese drum! I don't want to hear what they are saying!"

But the strange figures continued without mercy and death nodded his head, confirming everything they said.

"Music! Music!" shouted the emperor in desperation. "And you, my beloved golden nightingale, sing, sing as loud as you can! I have conferred on you the highest honors. I have always kept you next to me. So, sing, sing now!"

But the bird was silent, because there was no one to wind it up.

Death continued to loom silent and ominous above the emperor, looking at him with his horrible hollow orbits, brandishing the sword with one hand and holding his banner with the other.

At that moment, from the window came a marvelous song, and it spread throughout the room. It was the little nightingale of the woods who had heard from the fishermen of the great suffering that afflicted the emperor and had come to comfort him with her melodies and give him new hope. While she was singing, the disturbing shapes, peeping from the folds of the curtains, grew paler and paler, and their voices grew increasingly distant. The blood began to flow more strongly in the exhausted body of the emperor, giving him renewed vigor.

Even death listened to the sweet song in admiration, and he encouraged her not to stop, but to prolong her song with melodies that were ever new. "Go on, little Nightingale, go on," he said.

"Only if you give me your golden sword, and your rich banner. Only if you give me the emperor's crown!" replied the nightingale.

And death, without hesitation, gave her everything she asked for or in exchange for another song. The nightingale went on singing. She sang of the quiet churchyard where white roses were blooming, where the elder tree's perfume was delicate, where the grass was watered by the tears of those who mourned the loss of loved-ones. Then, death, assailed by a deep longing for his garden, floated like white fog out of the window. The emperor thanked the nightingale and told her, "My little friend, I imprisoned you and then I banished you from my kingdom, and yet you came to my rescue. You charmed away from my bed those evil visions, and you have driven death from my heart. How can I reward you? Ask me anything and it shall be yours!"

"I already have my reward," said the nightingale. "You gave me your tears the first time I sang to you: remember? I will never forget it! But now rest and get well. I will stay beside you and sing for you."

The following morning, when he woke up, the emperor was healed and full of energy. "Stay with me forever!" he begged the nightingale. "You shall sing only when it pleases you, and I will destroy the mechanical bird."

"Do not do it," said the nightingale. "Keep it with you. I cannot live in the palace, but I will come every night and sing for you, to give you the serenity to think of the good you can do for those who suffer and how you can remedy the injustices that are committed without your knowledge. I will come to sing for you, but you have to promise me something."

"Whatever you desire!" replied the emperor.

"Never tell anyone that I come every day to tell you what is happening in your kingdom." So saying, the nightingale flew away.

The emperor's servants entered the emperor's bedchamber that morning, believing him dead. Imagine their astonishment when he greeted them with a cheerful "Good morning!"

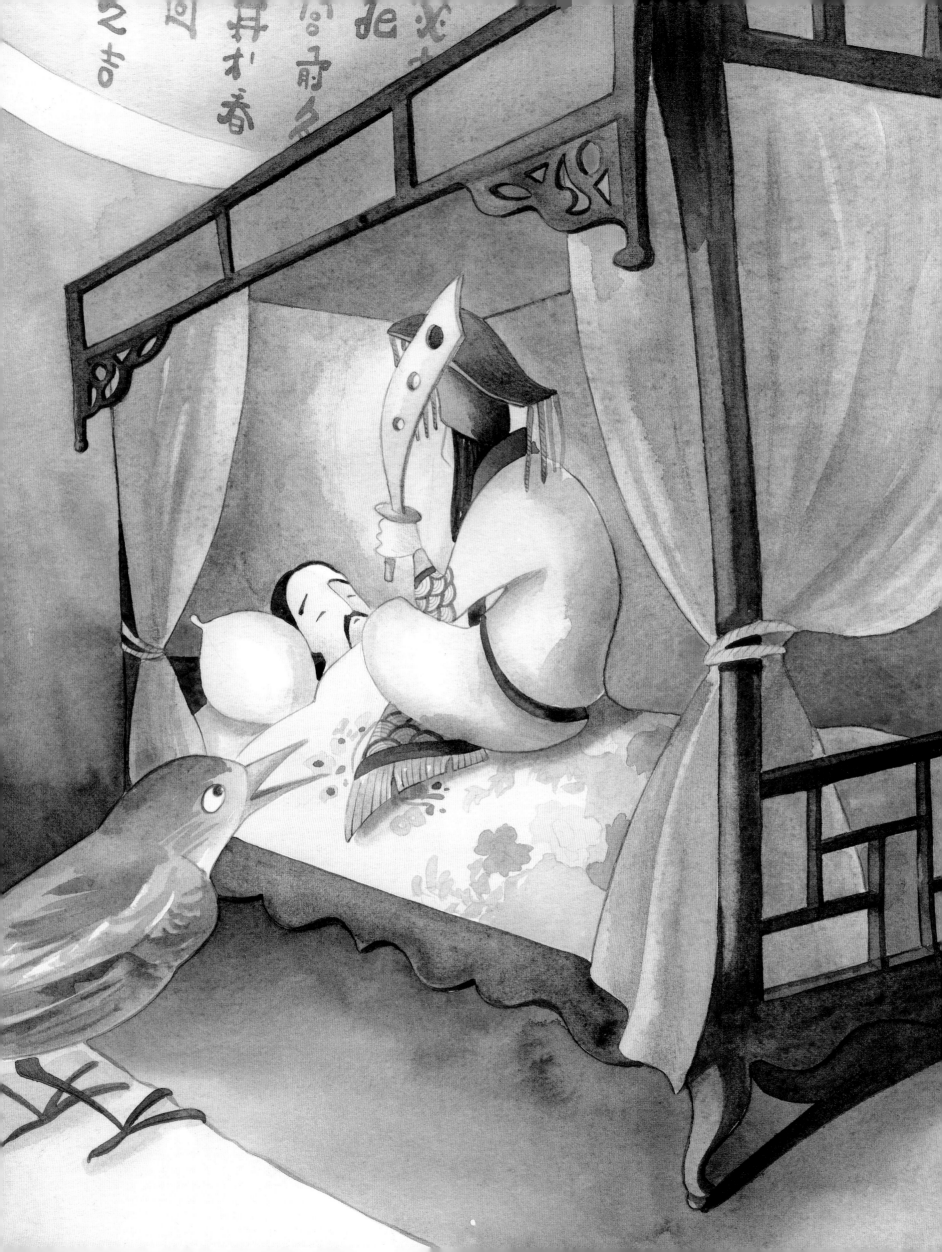

Thumbelina

There was once a woman who longed to have a child, but having lost all hope, she decided to resort to the magical arts of an old witch. So, she went to her to ask if she could help her realize her dream. "It is not complicated!" said the witch. "Here is a grain of barley. But mind, this is not a common grain such as those you give to the chickens. Plant it in a pot and you'll see that your wish will come true." After paying the old witch with the twelve coins they had agreed on, and having thanked her, she went home and planted the grain of barley in a beautiful pot. It was not long before a lovely flower appeared, like a tulip, but with its petals tightly closed. The woman was admiring it one day when, suddenly, she felt a tiny explosion and the petals opened up, revealing within them a very small girl child, very delicate and very graceful. Imagine the woman's surprise! In admiration, she looked closer at the child. She was no taller than a thumb, so the woman decided to call her Thumbelina.

She took a walnut shell and made it into a cradle, decorating it with colored patterns, making a mattress out of purple leaves and adding a rose petal as a cover. During the day, the girl played on the table, where the woman had placed a plate, which she had filled with water and decorated with fragrant flowers around the edge. A tulip petal served as a boat, and it amused Thumbelina to sail in it on the lake with the help of two horse hairs which she used as oars. It was a truly enchanting sight, and the child made it even more moving as she sang with a sweet and melodious voice. The days passed in complete serenity, and the woman felt happier than she had ever been in her life.

But one terrible night a big, slimy toad jumped in through the window and saw Thumbelina asleep in her walnut shell.

The toad was enchanted and thought Thumbelina would make the perfect bride for her son. So, she took the child as she slept, cradle and all, and returned to the pond at the bottom of the garden. The toad's son was just as ugly and slimy as his mother, and when he saw Thumbelina he croaked happily but in a most inelegant way: "Ribbet! Ribbet!" His mother scolded him: "Don't shout, you might wake her up and frighten her away. Let's put her nutshell on this big lily pad in the middle of the pond, surrounded by water, so that she cannot escape, while we go and prepare your new home." The following morning, when she awoke, the girl looked around bewildered, unable to figure out where he was. Frightened, she began to cry and tried in vain to find some way of escaping, but around her there was nothing but the dark water of the pond. Meanwhile, the mother toad and her son had completed their preparations. Now they saw that she was awake and swam to the leaf on which Thumbelina was crying desperately. Trying her best to soothe her, the mother toad said, "This is my son, your future husband. You will go and live with him at the bottom of the pond in the beautiful house we have prepared for you." Saying this, the two toads began to draw Thumbelina towards her new home. Meanwhile, the fish in the pond had witnessed the scene, and, curious about the new bride, they began to crowd around the leaf on which the little girl was still weeping. As soon as they saw her, they were enchanted by her grace and decided to help her escape this horrible fate. Quick as a flash, they swam down to the bottom of the pond and with their teeth began to saw at the stem of the lily until at last, freed of its anchor, it began to float across the water, carrying Thumbelina

away from her kidnappers. Now the little girl embarked on a long journey, cheered by the chirping of birds and accompanied by a lovely butterfly. To navigate more quickly, Thumbelina tied one end of her belt to the stem of the leaf and the other to the butterfly's waist. Soon, however, her journey was interrupted. A huge beetle, dived down on the child and, grabbing her with his feet, carried her away to a tree, while the lily pad floated on its way, taking the poor butterfly with it, still attached to its stem by the belt. Scared and desperate for her friend, Thumbelina lay on the highest leaf of the tree. The beetle brought her some pollen and then settled down to look at her. He was perplexed, for in her he could not see any resemblance to his own race. Other beetles arrived, and they all began to examine her carefully. "But it has only two legs," said one. "And it doesn't have any the antennas," noted another. "And not even wings!" exclaimed a third. "It's really ugly!" concluded a fourth. So, the beetle, while finding Thumbelina so pretty, was persuaded to give her up and he carried her to the foot of the tree, and deposited her on a daisy. All summer long the child lived alone in the woods, eating flower pollen and drinking the morning dew, but the summer passed quickly, and autumn came, and then came the winter. Now it was cold, it rained often and sometimes falling snowflakes were so big that they covered her completely. Thumbelina could not always find anything to eat, and dry leaves were not enough to keep her warm. Although she was by now weak, the girl decided to cross the vast wheat field - now frozen - that stretched out beyond the forest, to seek help. Thus, she came to the house of a little field mouse, who lived in a hole dug under the stubble. The house was very comfortable. There was a big kitchen, a cozy living room and an ample pantry full of grain. Thumbelina knocked on the door, and asked politely for

something to eat. The little mouse was immediately enchanted by the girl's grace and told her she could stay until winter's end, provided she would help her with the housework and tell good stories. Thumbelina accepted happily. One day she went to visit an old friend of the little mouse. It was Mr. Mole, who lived in a beautiful house close by. It had large rooms, an elegant lounge and a pantry full of food. In short, it was a party not to be missed! Mr. Mole, who could not see anything and who hated the sun and light, made a fine show of his soft black fur. He made sure they knew how wealthy he was and did his best to show off his wide knowledge. The little mouse asked Thumbelina to sing something, and Mr. Mole, hearing her sweet voice, fell in love with the girl. He told them he had just dug a tunnel that passed from his home to that of the little mouse and he invited them to visit whenever they wished. He added that they should not be frightened by the presence of a dead bird, which was harmless. Then he offered to accompany them, going ahead to show them the way. Reaching the dead bird, Mr. Mole made a hole in the ceiling of the tunnel to let a little light in. On the floor lay a poor, lifeless swallow. Thumbelina felt great pity for her, while their companion gave her a violent kick. That night the little girl could not sleep for thinking about the poor swallow, so she got up and ventured into the tunnel, taking with her some straw to cover it and keep it warm. As she stooped to stroke the soft feathers, Thumbelina felt the bird's heart beating feebly: the swallow was still alive! Thumbelina took care of her all winter. Secretly, she took her food and water, and healed the wound that she had received when she had fallen among the brambles, and which had prevented her from flying with her companions to warmer places at the end of the summer.

When spring came, the little girl opened the hole that Mr. Mole had made in the ceiling and freed her friend. The swallow offered to carry her away

on her back, but Thumbelina was grateful to the little mouse and did not want to leave her alone. So, the swallow flew away. The little mouse, for her part, had big plans for the little girl. She had decided that she should be given in marriage to Mr. Mole, and had already begun to make her trousseau. Thumbelina really did not want to, and often she gazed at the sky, hoping to see her friend the swallow. Autumn came and with it came their wedding day. The child was very sad. She could look forward to a life of boredom and darkness! She decided to say a final farewell to the sun and the light, and she went out into the open air, savoring the last few minutes of joy. It was at that moment that she heard the unmistakable fluttering of a swallow. It was her friend who, after listening to her story, asked her to fly away with her. This time without hesitation, Thumbelina sat on the back of the swallow and flew away with her toward the south. They crossed many wonderful lands and eventually stopped near a lake, on whose shores stood a magnificent marble palace. This was their destination. Here the swallow had her nest. She put Thumbelina down on a large lily and said goodbye. With amazement the little girl saw a little man, sitting on a flower. He was all white, transparent as glass. He had a shiny crown on his head and from his shoulders protruded two beautiful mother-of-pearl wings. It was the king of the lilies and all the tiny people who lived among them. The two fell in love at first sight and decided to get married. The day of the wedding, Thumbelina received as a gift two beautiful wings, which allowed her to fly freely from flower to flower. She was also given a new name: Maia. After the wedding, the swallow came to greet the new queen of lilies and then flew off to distant shores, bringing to the world the extraordinary story of Thumbelina.

Francesca Rossi

Born in 1983, she graduated from the International School of Comics in Florence. She publishes illustrated books with various Italian publishers and does drawings for covers and posters. In addition to illustrating, she offers educational workshops in schools and libraries, and creates and decorates ceramic art. For White Star Kids, she illustrated the "Classic Fairytales" series, "Who's Afraid of Witches? 100 Fun Activities for Brave Children", "Who's Afraid of the Big Bad Wolf? 100 Fun Activities for Brave Children", "Classic Fairy Tales by Charles Perrault", "Alice's Little Wonderlands, An Entertaining Coloring Experience", the titles "Fairy Tale Adventures", "Woodland Fairy Tales", "Princess Fairy Tales" in the Puzzle Book series, "Classic Fairy Tales by the Brothers Grimm", "Little Women" and "Around the World in Eighty Days".

Text adaptation
Valeria Manferto De Fabianis

Graphic design
Valentina Figus

WSkids
WHITE STAR KIDS

White Star Kids® is a registered trademark property of White Star s.r.l.

© 2017 White Star s.r.l.
Piazzale Luigi Cadorna, 6 - 20123 Milan, Italy
www.whitestar.it

Translation and Editing: Contextus Srl, Pavia (Louise Bostock)

ISBN 978-88-544-1102-9
1 2 3 4 5 6   21 20 19 18 17

Printed in China